Rocky Mountain Night Before Christmas

Rocky Mountain Night Before Christmas

By Joe Gribnau

Illustrated by
Salima Alikhan

PELICAN PUBLISHING COMPANY
GRETNA 2007

To my wife, Mell. Thanks for all your encouragement.—J. G.

For Ginster, Meg, Moogie, and Chop, my angels—S. A.

Copyright © 2007
By Joe Gribnau

Illustrations copyright © 2007
By Salima Alikhan

*The word "Pelican" and the depiction of a pelican
are trademarks of Pelican Publishing Company, Inc.,
and are registered in the U.S. Patent and Trademark Office.*

Library of Congress Cataloging-in-Publication Data

Gribnau, Joe.
  Rocky Mountain night before Christmas / Joe Gribnau; illus-
trated by Salima Alikhan.
     p. cm.
  Based on Clement Moore's Night before Christmas.
  ISBN 978-1-58980-317-6 (alk. paper)
 1. Cowboys—Juvenile poetry. 2. Santa Claus—Juvenile poetry.
3. Rocky Mountains—Juvenile poetry. 4. Christmas stories. 5.
Children's poetry, American. I. Alikhan, Salima, ill. II. Moore,
Clement Clarke, 1779-1863. Night before Christmas. III. Title.
  PS3607.R523R63 2007
  811'.6--dc22

                                            2007011737

Printed in Singapore
Published by Pelican Publishing Company, Inc.
1000 Burmaster Street, Gretna, Louisiana 70053

Rocky Mountain Night Before Christmas

On a cold winter's night, ridin' in from the plains,
The cattle all bedded, I lay a light grip on the reins.
Snow snakes were twistin', blowin' hard from the north;
My lashes were frozen, so I gave lead to my horse.

Buckin' through drifts and fightin' the cold—
A Rocky Mountain winter is a sight to behold.

Ridin' up on my cabin, I couldn't figure this out:
Lashed to a sleigh, eight cows milled about.

I had just left my bunch west of Dry Crick;
This was either a rustler or a darn dirty trick.

Then my cuttin' horse snorted, sidestepped, and shied
As a big, fat red feller on the rooftop I spied.
With a spit of my chaw and a flick of my wrist,
I rolled out a nice loop and roped him right quick.

Then down off the rooftop he slid with a holler;
My horse held him tight as I grabbed his fur collar.

A cattle thief's justice in the Rockies, you see,
Is from the back of a horse with a noose and a tree.

But he looked vaguely familiar from my childhood days—
The red britches, black boots, and a jolly old gaze.

So I eased up my grip as he lay in the snow,
And he laughed with a wink and said, "Please, let me go."

Well, I got to figurin' who was makin' such fuss,
Tipped back my Stetson, and started to cuss.

"You're lucky tonight, my fat little friend;
If it weren't for the suit, you'd be seein' the end."

In the warmth of my cabin, we had us a nip—
Takes the chill off the night and soothes my bad hip.

I told him stories of my cowboyin' days
Workin' for food and not enough pay.

I started my herd on the slopes of the Crazies,
Where the bear grass blooms in fields full of daisies.

It's been a hard life, lots of toil and sweat,
But it's one that I chose without any regret.

You can have the big cities with their glitter and gold,
Just give me a cow horse and a saddle to hold.
Here in the Rockies we're part of the land,
A true place of splendor by the Almighty's hand.

He listened and nodded, then said, "I must go,"
Shouldered his satchel, sauntered out in the snow.

Then tipping his hat, he jumped in the sleigh
And called to each cow as he went on his way:

Up Bullet and Babe, up Shorty and Slim,
Molly and Mary, Old Jed and Big Jim.

Away in the night they left not a track,
And somehow I knew he wouldn't be back.

But warm in my cabin, a little more for the wise,
I noticed a package to my merry surprise.
With the spittoon ringin', I stared at my loot:
A straight-brimmed Stetson and alligator boots.

I felt sort of giddy and light in the head,
And liked 'em so much, I wore 'em to bed.

And just before shuttin' my tired eyes tight,
I heard "May your trail be easy and your burden be light!"